The Porcelain Man

The Porcelain Man

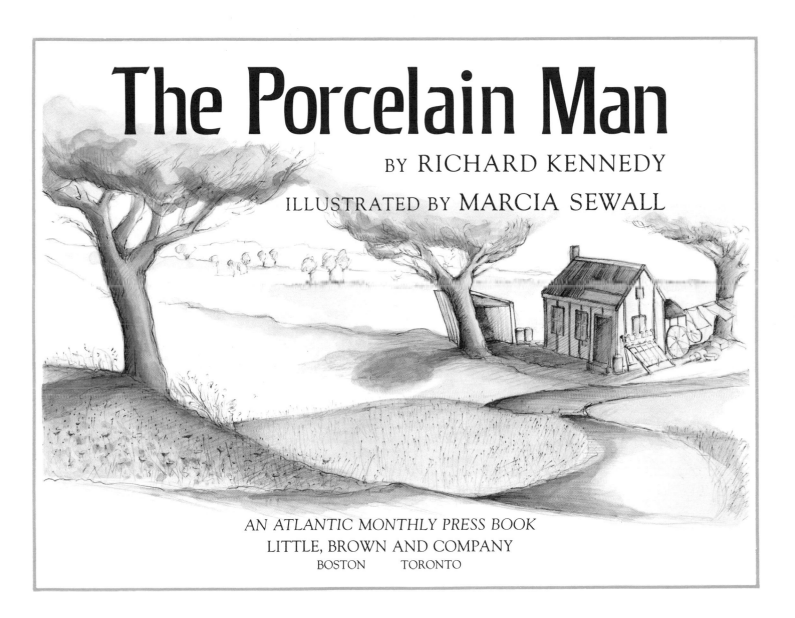

BY RICHARD KENNEDY

ILLUSTRATED BY MARCIA SEWALL

AN ATLANTIC MONTHLY PRESS BOOK

LITTLE, BROWN AND COMPANY

BOSTON   TORONTO

Books by Richard Kennedy

THE PARROT AND THE THIEF

THE CONTESTS AT COWLICK

THE PORCELAIN MAN

FIRST EDITION

T 05/76

ATLANTIC-LITTLE, BROWN BOOKS
ARE PUBLISHED BY
LITTLE, BROWN AND COMPANY
IN ASSOCIATION WITH
THE ATLANTIC MONTHLY PRESS

Library of Congress Cataloging in Publication Data

Kennedy, Richard.
    The porcelain man.

    "An Atlantic Monthly Press book."
    SUMMARY: Everytime the poor girl mends the
broken porcelain vase it becomes something different,
providing the means of escaping from her dreary
existence of mending junk.
    [1. Fairy tales]   I. Sewall, Marcia.   II. Title.
PZ8.K387Po   [E]   75-25783
ISBN 0-316-48901-8

*Published simultaneously in Canada
by Little, Brown & Company (Canada) Limited*

PRINTED IN THE UNITED STATES OF AMERICA

For my mother

ONCE UPON A TIME at the edge of town lived a harsh man with a timid daughter who had grown pale and dreamy from too much obedience. The man kept the girl busy and hardly ever let her go out of doors. "You're lucky to be inside where it's safe and sound," he would say to her. "It's dog-eat-dog out there. The world is full of bottle-snatchers, ragmongers, and ratrobbers. Believe you me!"

The girl believed him.

Each morning the man left the house in his rickety wagon pulled by his rackety horse. All day long he would go up and down the streets of the town, into the countryside and to neighboring villages to find what he could find. He would bring home old broken wheels, tables and chairs with the legs gone from them, pots and pans with holes in them, scraps of this and pieces of that. His daughter would then mend and repair the junk during her long and lonely days inside the house, and the man would take the things away and sell them as secondhand goods. This is the way they lived.

One morning the man left the house and gave his daughter his usual instruction and warning. "If someone passes on the road, stay away from the windows. If someone knocks, don't answer. I could tell you terrible stories." Then he left, and the girl began work on a broken lantern.

Now this morning some good luck happened to the man. As he was passing a rich man's house, a clumsy kitchen maid chased two cats out the front door with a broom and knocked over a large porcelain vase. The vase rolled out the door and down the steps and path, and shattered to pieces against a marble pillar near the roadway. The man stopped, and watched. The maid closed the

door. The man waited there for ten minutes. No one came out. Then he leaped down from his cart and gathered up the broken porcelain. He set the pieces gently in his cart and hurried off toward home.

His daughter, as usual, was safe and sound inside. "This is fine porcelain," the man said. "Drop whatever you're doing and patch it up. We'll get a good price for it."

It was early in the day yet, so the man left again to see what else he might find. He remembered to pause at the door and say, "Stay inside. Terrible things are going on out there. Dog-eat-dog, the devil take the hindmost, and so forth." Then he left.

The girl turned a piece of porcelain in her fingers, admiring its beauty. She carefully laid the pieces on a blanket and got out the glue. Then, humming to herself and musing on fanciful thoughts in the way she had acquired from being so much alone, she began to put the pieces of porcelain together. She worked quickly and neatly even though her thoughts were completely elsewhere, and at the end of a couple of hours she was amazed to see that she had just set the last piece in place on a full-sized porcelain man. And at that moment the porcelain man spoke.

"I love you," he said, taking a step toward the girl.

"Gracious!" gasped the girl, snatching up the blanket and throwing it about the man. "Gracious!" she gasped again as the porcelain man encircled her in his arms and kissed her.

While this was happening, the girl's father returned to the house. And right at this moment he opened the door to the room.

"Whoa!" he bellowed.

He grabbed a chair, raised it above his head and brought it down

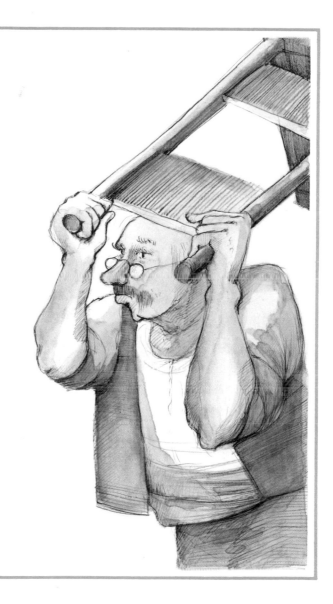

squarely on top of the head of the porcelain man with a blow that shattered him from head to toe, and the porcelain pieces scattered over the floor.

"Godamighty!" the man cried, "I've fractured his skull!" The girl let out a wail, and the man dropped to his knees, stunned with the catastrophe. But the girl explained that it had not been a real man, but only one made of the porcelain.

"A porcelain man who could move!?"

"And he could talk as well," said the girl.

"Fantastic!" said the man. "Quick, put him together again before you forget how you did it. I'll make a cage for him and take him to the county fair. I'll charge a dollar to see him. He can learn to dance. I'll make a big sign saying, 'See the dancing pot,' or something like that. I'll make thousands! Quick, put him together again!"

So the girl collected the pieces on the blanket and slowly began gluing them together again. Her father sat down and watched her for a while, but he found it to be boring and he dropped off to sleep.

The girl worked on, very sad that the porcelain man would be taken away in a cage. She was so distressed by her thoughts that she did not notice until putting the last piece in place that she had built a small porcelain horse. And the horse neighed.

The man woke up.

"What's that?" he said. "That's no man, that's a horse. Now you'll just have to do it all over again. And this time, *concentrate!*" Saying this, the man took up the chair over his head so as to smash the horse.

But the horse said to the girl, "Quickly, jump on my back!" She did, and in a second the horse leaped out of the window with the girl, and they galloped across the countryside as the man stood waving the chair at them through the window and shouting words they could not hear.

20

After running for several miles, the horse stopped in a small meadow in the center of which stood a tree.

"Get down," said the horse. The girl did. "Now," said the horse, "I will run into the tree and break myself to pieces, and then you are to put me back together as a man again." Then the horse added, "Remember — I love you," and before

the girl could say a word, the horse dashed toward the tree and crashed into it at full gallop and broke into hundreds of pieces.

The girl cried out, and then sat down under the tree and wept, for she had no glue.

Now on a path nearby came along a young man pushing a wheelbarrow. He stopped when he saw the girl by the tree, and went to comfort her.

"Don't cry," he said. "Here, let us gather up the pieces and put them in the wheelbarrow. Come along with me and we'll fix everything almost as good as new."

So they loaded up the broken porcelain, and they went to the man's cottage and spread the pieces out on a blanket.

"It must have been a beautiful set of dishes," said the man, and he began to glue some pieces together. They talked as they worked and told each other all about themselves. The girl admired how well and quickly the young man worked with his hands, and in a short while they had put together a dozen dishes, eight saucers and teacups, six bowls, two large serving platters, a milk pitcher and two small vases.

They cooked supper then. Their eyes met often as they moved about. Now and again their hands touched, and they brushed against each other as they moved about.

They set the table with the porcelain ware, and when they were eating the girl's plate whispered up at her, "I still love you."

"Hush!" she said.

"I beg your pardon?" the young man said.

"Oh, nothing," said the girl.

And they lived happily ever after.